Newton Primary School

COLOUR JETS

# DAD ON THE RUN

## Sarah Garland

Collins

## COLOUR JETS

| | |
|---|---|
| *Dad on the Run* | Sarah Garland |
| *Stinker Muggles and the Dazzle Bug* | Elizabeth Laird |
| *Francis Fry, Private Eye* | Sam McBratney |
| *Even Stevens F.C.* | Michael Rosen |

First published in Great Britain by
HarperCollins Publishers Ltd 1995

9 8 7 6 5 4 3 2

Text & illustrations © Sarah Garland 1995

A CIP record for this title is available
from the British Library.

ISBN 0 00 675009-5

**Printed and bound in Italy**

# Chapter 1
## A Big Problem

"It's your turn," said Mum. And she was out of the door as Dad opened his mouth for his first spoonful of cornflakes.

"Not the SCHOOL RUN!" he choked.

But Mum was gone.

I was on the doormat with Mackenzie and all our school gear, and my tenor sax and Mack's model of an Ancient Egyptian pyramid.

"We're ready," I said.

"Well I'm not," said Dad, chewing faster.

"You've *got* to come now," said Mackenzie, "because my class is doing Assembly."

"And it's our day for collecting Spitt. And it's the concert," I said.

Slrmph!

"But I'm
not dressed," said Dad,
beginning to look rather wild.
"Just put this anorak on and come,"
said Mackenzie.

She got an anorak from behind the door and his car key from the hook.

"Beano! My hair!" said Dad.

"Forget it," I said. "You look fine. Anyway, no one will see. And there's not much of it," I added.

Thllpp!

Horrible boy!

Mackenzie put Dad's anorak on over his pyjamas.

"Feet!" said Dad, taking a gulp of tea.

Mackenzie looked around. Under the table were Mum's slippers. She put them on Dad's feet.

I opened the door. Dad staggered out into the drizzling morning, toast in one hand, car key in the other.

"Don't worry. You'll be back again before you can say Weetabix," I said.

Weetabix

Spitt was on the corner, one arm round his guitar, the other waving and pointing to a figure beside him.

"Who's that?" said Dad, peering through the misting windscreen. "Where are my blasted glasses?"

"Looks like Spitt's mum," I said doubtfully.

It *was* Mrs Pitt. She was in rather an odd position, bending over a low wall with her weight on her hands, her long hair hanging down, all draggly in the rain.

Spitt put his head in through the window. He looked like a red-faced hunting trophy on a wall. His voice was strained.

Could you give Mum a lift, Mr Baxter?
She's started having the baby!
I rang Dad at work and he's meeting us at school and taking her to hospital!

"Can't talk. Got to concentrate," said Mrs Pitt, easing her large body on to the front seat.

She was breathing heavily and counting. Dad tried to do up her safety belt, but it wouldn't go.

In... two... three... Out... two... three...

What with her and Spitt's guitar, and my tenor sax and all of us, the car was very full. Its engine soon began to whine in an unhealthy way. The windows were completely misted up.

Dad kept saying inane
things, like "Have you there in a jiffy,
Mrs Pitt," and "Hang on in there,
Mrs Pitt." And whenever we stopped at
traffic lights he drummed on the
steering wheel and looked slightly
desperately at us in the rear mirror.

We sat quietly, not like most mornings.
Even Mackenzie was subdued. We just
listened to Mrs Pitt's breathing, which
was quite loud.

## Chapter 2
## Nightmare!

For once I was really pleased to get to school.

"Remember to come to the concert at two o'clock Dad," I said, as we pushed and shoved each other out of the car.

Mrs Pitt began to heave herself up. Dad got out to help her.

"Oh Dad!" I groaned.

The hordes of children streaming up the pavement towards us looked sideways at Dad, then ran sniggering through the school gate.

I felt furious with them, and protective towards Dad who was bending so kindly over Mrs Pitt. But at the same time I was *furious* with him for looking such an idiot.

There was a sudden
turmoil in the crowd.
A small man was
fighting his way
through. He was the
image of Spitt, with
a reddish moustache.
He was shouting like
a sergeant major.

Oy!

BELLA!
BELLA!
GET BACK IN!

Mrs Pitt fell immediately
and heavily back into
the front seat.

Dad looked round
in surprise.

Mr Pitt darted past
him, round the car and
into the driving seat.
He turned the key,
revved the engine.

Very sorry, old man. Flat battery in the Sierra! Emergency! Back in a shake!

Mrs Pitt mouthed something through the window at Spitt and waved goodbye, her face all blurry through the rain.
Then they were gone.

Blue exhaust fumes drifted in the gutter.

We were shocked speechless.

It had all happened so fast.

And there was Dad, dazed, stranded seven miles from home, teetering on his little heels in the rain.

She herded us through the gates. We pressed closely round Dad to shield his lower half – the grubby pyjamas, the terrible slippers.

"You *can't* Dad!"
hissed Mackenzie
desperately.

"No. I can't,"
agreed Dad.
He seemed
strangely
calm.

"What a horrible dream this is," he said. "But then, everybody has nightmares about talking to headmistresses while wearing their pyjamas… "

"Especially when their pyjamas are falling down because they've lost the safety pin," he added, clutching at his waist and smiling around him in a vague and peculiar way.

In a few seconds we would be
through the door. Ms Green
was ahead as we passed
the bike shed.
A voice in my head said,
*"NOW OR NEVER."*
"In there," I said.

We wheeled to the
right, still pressed
together like a well-
drilled army unit,
ducked into the
bike shed and fell
weakly against
the wall.

## Chapter 3
## Inspiration!

Through the grimy bike shed window I watched Ms Green as she turned at the school door to welcome us in.

She paused in surprise.

She peered around the playground.

Finally she shook the raindrops off her umbrella and disappeared inside.

"Beano," said Dad. "It *is* a nightmare, isn't it?"

"What do you think, Spitt?" I asked.

"I don't think it is," said Spitt. "I can feel the rain dripping down inside my collar."

"It definitely isn't," said Mackenzie. "It hurts when I pinch myself. My Assembly starts in three minutes. Just stay here till break, Dad. Mr Pitt might come back with the car any minute."

"But it takes ages to have a baby," said Dad, faintly. I could see he was beginning to realise that the bike shed was not a dream but hard, damp concrete.

"It's not long, Dad," I said. "We *must* go. I'll think of something by break. Really."

I felt awful leaving him. I heard him murmur, "Yeah. Before you can say Weetabix," as we collected our bags and ran to join the last stragglers through the main school door.

Help me, Beano!

My mind drifted away.
I thought of Mum sitting,
neat and tidy
at her office
desk, sipping
her first
cup of coffee
of the day.

Then I
thought of
Dad crouching
damp and
huddled, in the
bike shed.

Now Ms Green had pinned up a big picture of a carved blue cat, and was telling us

HOW EGYPTIANS HAD WORSHIPPED CATS,

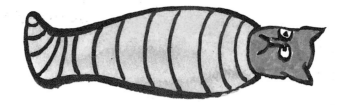

AND MUMMIFIED THEM WHEN THEY DIED,

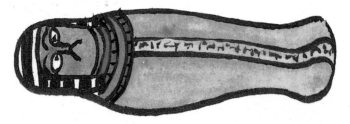

AND BURIED THEM IN PAINTED COFFINS.

"And here is my own beautiful cat, called Nefertiti after the Egyptian queen. See how like an Egyptian cat she is," said Ms Green. She lifted up a big Siamese with rather spooky crossed eyes.

"She's so sensitive and clever. It's easy to imagine the Ancient Egyptians thinking she's a goddess, isn't it?"

"A witch more like," muttered Spitt.

"And I want you to be extra quiet near my study today, so she isn't disturbed," said Ms Green. "She's very highly strung. Aren't you, poppet?"

Under cover of the hymn (*Father Hear the Prayers We Offer*), Spitt sang,

Shoes and trousers there must be

I joined in, out of tune and cracking on the high notes,

But wherever can we find them?

and Spitt answered,

Our first lesson is P.E.

Of course. We all had to change for P.E. and old Gibbo, the P.E. teacher, did too. We'd just borrow his shoes and trousers, and get them out to Dad at break.

A doddle!

So when we passed Mackenzie in the corridor on the way to the gym I said, with all the confidence in the world, "It's sorted, Mac. See you at break."

Great, Beano! See ya!

## Chapter 4
## Who is Rosebud?

Gibbo had his own room behind a curtain off the gym, where he brewed herbal tea, practised weightlifting and kept his tracksuits.

We began jogging five times round the gym. Each time we passed the room I looked greedily in at a pair of trousers on a hanger, and at the trainers under a chair. I nudged Spitt.

"Class HALT!" shouted Gibbo. "Into teams for kingball, one two, quick march."

"I'll be king," I said hastily to my team. They all agreed, because I'm so tall that I'm good on the back line. (My name is short for Beanpole.)

Ready team?

"Good thinking," said Spitt, reading my mind.

I ran to take up my position behind the line, in front of Gibbo's room, and began to bounce about, looking keen.

Gibbo looked surprised. I'm not usually enthusiastic about gym.

He was even more surprised at Spitt, who is totally unathletic but who leaped eagerly at the ball whenever it came near him, and was hit at last in the chest.

Spitt cast a meaningful look at me as he fell heavily to the floor.

Oh! Mr Gibson! Ouch!

As Gibbo bent over him, I darted into the room and reached for the trousers.

RRRRRRRRRRRRRR

My hand froze in mid-air.

The floor was shaking, the air vibrating.

I looked round wildly.

An earthquake?

In the gym?

No! It was Gibbo's Rosebud, her jaws slavering, about to give a ferocious howl!

I snatched my hand back, making a high-pitched, trembling noise that was meant to sound like, "Easy Boy!"

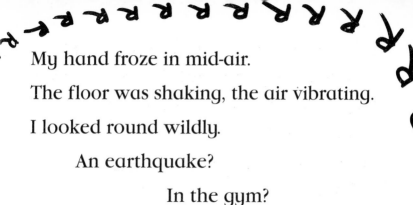

GGGGGGRR

eeeeeeeezzoy...

In a flash I was back in the gym, dancing behind the line, with sweat trickling down inside my games shirt.

Gibbo was straightening up, saying, "Ridiculous fuss, Pitt."

Spitt joined me, hissing, "Well?"

"No good. I forgot Rosebud," I panted, jumping for the ball and hurling it the length of the gym. I could feel the blood racing round my body, giving me the strength of ten.

"Well played Baxter," approved Gibbo.

Behind me I heard a low but powerful, growl.

Art was next. We all sighed because we had been doing the same still life for a fortnight.

It was only halfway through the lesson that I realised I was painting a tasty lunch. Dad would be pleased!

I waited until everyone had gone, then slipped the pie and celery into my bag. The celery was a bit droopy, but I didn't think Dad would mind.

I jumped about two feet when Mr Morgan came back into the room.

So did he. He'd been hoping for a quiet smoke.

39

aaaagh

**DEATH BY FOOD POISONING**

John Baxter, father of two, and only 38 years old, died today after eating a very old pork pie, given to him by his son Benjamin (known to his friends as Beano).

Then he looked around. "Baxter! Where's the still life?" he growled. "Wait! I can smell it!"

He opened my bag and pulled out the crumbling pie.

"Yerk, Baxter! You weren't going to *eat* it, were you?"

Then his voice softened. "Poor chap. Have some chocolate and run along to break."

In the bike shed Dad was even more dishevelled now, almost like a tramp. His stubble was bluer. His horny toe nails poked, curving and yellow, from the pink furry slippers.

I gave him the chocolate.

"Is that all?" he demanded.

"I did try," I said. "I nearly got you a pork pie in Art, but Mr Morgan came in. And I nearly got you trousers and shoes in Gym, but there was this very fierce dog..."

"I *suppose* it wasn't worth you being savaged to death," said Dad gloomily.

Mackenzie was impatient. "Can't you just *walk* home, Dad?" she said.

"I can't face it," said Dad. "Seven miles looking like this! I am a house father. I have my standards and my pride." His voice rose.

"Er… what are you going to call the new baby?" I asked Spitt hurriedly.

"We haven't decided yet," said Spitt.

So we all thought of names.

Mackenzie thought

I thought

Dad said, "How about Cess?" which showed what a bad state of mind he was in.

Then the bell went. We promised to come back at lunchtime.

"We'll bring you some of ours," said Spitt kindly.

In fact, Spitt and I had to spend most of lunchtime getting ready for the concert, so Mackenzie had to look after Dad on her own.

We each sent him a sandwich, and half a bag of crisps.

By now I had almost given up hope of rescuing Dad from the bike shed before the end of the school day, and was beginning to wonder how we were going to get him home at all.

# Chapter 5
## Bloodlust!

Now I had to concentrate with all my strength on my tenor sax piece. I had a solo part which was quite difficult.

Half the school is in the orchestra because Ms Green is so keen on music.

The audience began to file in, shuffling, coughing and shaking their hats and mackintoshes as the rain was belting down.

For an instant I thought about Dad
getting wet, but I was also getting very
nervous about my solo. My heart
seemed to be beating high up,
somewhere in my neck.

I wished Mum
could have come.
I wished Dad
was there, all
smart and clean,
in his suit.

I wished I'd practised
my solo last night
instead of watching
the telly.

I sucked my
reed and wiped
my slippery hands
on my trousers.

I realised then that
Ms Green must have
introduced my piece.

She raised her arms,
lifted her eyebrows, and
glanced encouragingly at me.

The hall was hushed.

I took a breath from deep in my chest
and began to play. My fingers knew, by
some miracle, what to do.

I let them do it.

Concentrated on my breathing.

Ahead was the moment when the orchestra would join in on a sharp, lifting run, and my part would be nearly over.

And then – then –
as the orchestra were poised
around me, waiting for the
downsweep of the baton –
there was a horrible scream!
A roaring, snarling howl!
And the double doors
at the end of the hall
burst open.

A pale ball of fury hurtled
down the aisle. It was Nefertiti,
every hair on end, crying an unearthly,
yowling cry.

After her raced Rosebud, his broken
chain whipping across
the floor, his eyes red
with bloodlust!

And after him –
Dad! Yes, Dad!
His anorak half
off, one hand
clutching his
pyjama trousers,
his hair wild
around
his head.

Dad leaping for Rosebud's chain as it
curved through the air.

Dad grabbing for
the harness, skidding
along the floor
in his furry pink slippers,
until the dog, with a
strangled snarl, was pulled
back on his haunches.

With a final screech, Nefertiti flung herself straight at Ms Green's bosom and stuck there, like Velcro, quivering.

Gibbo was scarlet-faced, snatching for his dog and dragging him from the hall.

The orchestra was transfixed.

Dad rose uncertainly to his feet. He looked around.

He smoothed his hair with a
trembling hand.

There was a
dreadful
silence.

# Chapter 6
## The Hero!

You are a HERO, Mr Baxter!

With one bound Ms Green leapt from the stage and grasped Dad by the hand.

She led him to a seat in the front row, dumped Nefertiti in his lap and clapped her hands.

"Back to your places, please!" She turned to us and lifted her baton.

Off we go!

And off we went.
It was a terrific concert.
We gave it all we had.
And when we ended with
*The Saints Go Marching In*
we nearly blew the roof off.

We had to
take five bows,
all of us. Ms Green
made me take an extra one because of
my solo, and Dad went on clapping
after everyone else had stopped.

As the audience began to leave,
I jumped from the stage to sit beside
Dad.

"That was fantastic Beano," he said.
"I'm glad I didn't miss it all."

Mackenzie came, and Spitt, and
Ms Green sat down with us with
Nefertiti on her lap.

"What happened, Dad?" I asked.

"I was in the bike
shed trying to
listen to the
concert, but the
rain and wind
were making a
terrible noise."

"Then there was
a big bang.
I looked out and
saw that Siamese
cat jump out of
a window."

"It made a beeline for the art room and disappeared inside. Then it re-appeared with some sort of pie in its mouth."

The still life!

"There was an awful screeching howl, then, from the gym and this… creature…like a hound from hell… came tearing out," said Dad. "When it saw the cat it went berserk. Twice round the playground they went with me after them, then into the hall. I didn't even think. I just kept going…"

"Thank heavens," said Ms Green, stroking Nefertiti, "or my poppet would most certainly be dead."

"But it was very embarrassing," said Dad ruefully.

"I think it made for a truly memorable concert," said Ms Green.

"Now Samuel," she said, (meaning Spitt) "there's good news for you. Your little sister has been born and your mum is well. I'm to take you home with the Baxters, to wait for your father."

A sister!

Spitt and I yelled and punched the air.
We all got into Ms Green's car.

Somehow Dad managed to look quite
dignified. He walked proudly.

He seemed to have got the hang of high
heels at last.

"Boiled eggs for everybody?" called Mackenzie from the kitchen. "You have a rest, Dad. I'll do it."

And that's how Mum found us when she came in half an hour later. She was outraged.

"I just can't believe this!" she stormed. "I've been working so *hard* all day, and here you all are still eating breakfast. The house is a disgusting mess! And honestly! John!" she cried. "You haven't even got dressed yet!"